I LOVE YOU
Verses & Sweet Sayings

featuring the art of
BESSIE PEASE GUTMANN

· GROSSET & DUNLAP ·

Contents

GOOD MORROW TO YOU,
VALENTINE

Good morrow to you, Valentine.
    Curl your locks as I do mine—
Two before and three behind.
    Good morrow to you, Valentine!

LITTLE MISS

Little miss, pretty miss,
    Blessings light upon you!
If I had half a crown a day,
    I'd spend it all upon you.

LAVENDER'S BLUE

Lavender's blue, dilly-dilly,
    Lavender's green;
When I am king, dilly-dilly,
    You shall be queen.

Let the birds sing, dilly-dilly,
    And the lambs play;
We shall be safe, dilly-dilly,
    Out of harm's way.

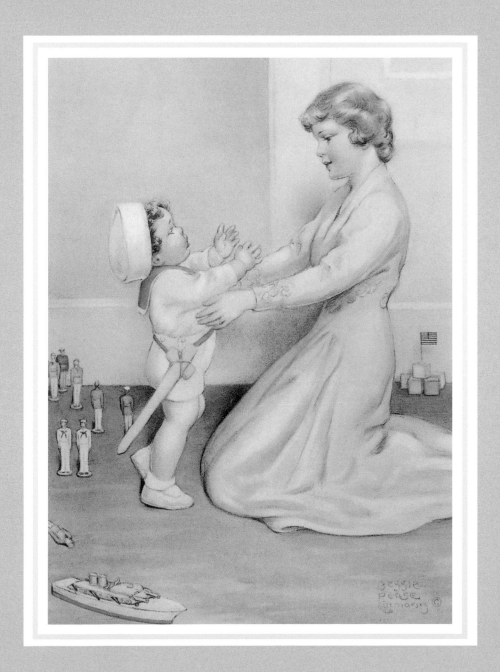

BEST FRIENDS

I've often thought that I would send
   A valentine to some dear friend.
Now, though I've many friends, 'tis true,
   My preference is all for you.
For if the truth must be confessed,
   Believe me, I love you the best!

I LOVE LITTLE PUSSY

I love little Pussy,
 Her coat is so warm;
And if I don't hurt her,
 She'll do me no harm.

So I'll not pull her tail,
 Or drive her away;
But Pussy and I
 Very gently will play.

She will sit by my side,
 And I'll give her some food;
And Pussy will love me
 Because I am good.

I never will vex her,
 Or make her displeased;
For Puss doesn't like
 To be worried or teased.

–Jane Taylor

MOTHER

Hundreds of stars in the deep blue sky,
    Hundreds of shells on the shore together,
Hundreds of birds that go singing by,
    Hundreds of birds in the sunny weather.

Hundreds of dewdrops to greet the dawn,
    Hundreds of bees in the purple clover,
Hundreds of butterflies on the lawn,
    But only one mother the wide world over.

–*George Cooper*

DO YOU LOVE ME?

Do you love me,
    Or do you not?
You told me once,
    But I forgot.

A SECRET

Somebody loves you
    Deep and true;
If I weren't so shy
    I'd tell you who!

CURLY LOCKS

Curly Locks, Curly Locks!
　　Wilt thou be mine?
Thou shalt not wash dishes
　　Or yet feed the swine,
But sit on a cushion
　　And sew a fine seam,
And feed upon strawberries,
　　Sugar, and cream.

NO FRIEND LIKE A SISTER

There is no friend like a sister
   In calm or stormy weather;
To cheer one on the tedious way,
   To fetch one if one goes astray,
To lift one if one totters down,
   To strengthen whilst one stands.

–Christina Rossetti

LOVE

Love to faults is always blind,
Always is to joy inclined,
Lawless, winged, and unconfined;
And breaks all chains from every mind.

–William Blake

IF APPLES WERE PEARS

If apples were pears,
And peaches were plums,
And the rose had a different name,
If tigers were bears,
And fingers were thumbs,
I'd love you just the same!

HE PRAYETH BEST

He prayeth best who loveth best
   All things both great and small;
For the dear God who loveth us,
   He made and loveth all.

        –Samuel Taylor Coleridge

FOR LOVE

Do all the good you can,
In all the ways you can,
In all the places you can,
At all the times you can,
To all the people you can,
As long as ever you can.

–John Wesley

SILVER AND GOLD

Make new friends,
   But keep the old.
One is silver,
   The other gold.